JE

Tinker Bell's Tea Party

By Lara Bergen and A. Picksey

Illustrated by the Disney Storybook Artists

New York
An Imprint of Disney Book Group

JUN 3 0 2009

Designed by Winnie Ho

Printed in Singapore

First Edition

1 3 5 7 9 10 8 6 4 2

Library of Congress Catalog Card Number on file.
ISBN 978-1-4231-0949-5

Visit www.DisneyFairies.com

It was only the middle of the morning, and Tinker Bell had finished all of her repairs.

She looked around her cozy, cluttered workshop, and her eye fell on a piece of Never silver. She had been saving it for a special occasion. There was just enough to make . . .

"A pretty silver teacup!" Tink said out loud. "Perfect!"

She went to work.

Soon enough, Tink had made herself a bright, beautiful little teacup. When she tapped it lightly with her hammer, it rang like a bell. She flew off to the tearoom to ask for some tea.

"Tea?" said Willow, a table-setting-talent fairy. She laughed. "Before lunch? Fairy dust! Everyone's so busy, you'll have to make it yourself."

The pots-and-pans talents believe it's good luck to drink tea out of a Never-silver cup.

Tink took a kettle and flew to Havendish Stream for water. There, she met her friend Rani, a water-talent fairy. Tink showed the silver cup she had made. "I'm going to make my own tea," she said.

"Oh!" cried Rani, "For a cup that pretty, you should have special tea—made with morning dew."

Rani led Tinker Bell to their friend Lily's garden, where the flowers still glistened with clear, sweet dew.

"Be careful," Lily warned Tink as they filled the kettle with sparkling dewdrops. "Sometimes these snapdragons really *do* snap!"

The language of snapdragons is easy for garden-talent fairies to learn, since these plants only say two things: "I am biting something!" and "I wish I were biting something!"

13

At that moment, one flower bent over and nipped at Tinker Bell's hair. Tink yelped.

Lily heard the noise and hurried over. She stroked the plant's leaves until it let go of Tink's ponytail. "You know," Lily said, "four-leaf-clover honey goes perfectly with dewdrop tea."

Tink felt a little impatient, but Rani was already whistling for Brother Dove to fly her to the clover patch. Rani had no wings and so Brother Dove helped her fly.

Tinker Bell, Rani, and Lily all followed Lily's bee friend, Bumble, past the orchard and the dust mill, and across marigold meadow.

Of all the honey in Pixie Hollow, four-leaf-clover honey has the finest taste and consistency. But it is so rare that the fairies use it only on special occasions.

Honeysuckle honey is extremely sweet and used only for baking.

Apple-blossom honey is used in most recipes—and also sometimes as glue.

Bumble persuaded the bees to give the fairies a generous drop of four-leaf-clover honey. Tink was just leaving to go start the tea when Beck, an animal-talent fairy, appeared.

"What's the special occasion?" Beck asked.

"Tink is making a special tea!" said Lily.

"Steeped in morning dew!" said Rani.

"With four-leaf-clover honey!" added Lily.

"What a treat," said Beck. "Are you having lavender cream with it, too?"

"You know," Tink said, "I'm sure it will be very nice with regular cream. Why don't we—"

"To the dairy barn, fairies," Rani interrupted her. "Hurry!"

"Mmm," Beck said with a sigh. "Tink's tea is going to be good!"

"If I ever get to have it," Tink muttered. She was glad her friends were so excited, but she *really* wanted to have her tea now.

The mice of Pixie Hollow provide wool and milk to the fairies.

Lavender-scented milk comes from mice who graze in the lavender meadow. It is strongly flavored, but perfect in a cup of fairy tea.

Mouse cheese is made from the milk of mice who graze in the sweetgrass meadow. The best butter comes from those mice who eat buttercup blossoms.

"All right," Tink said, as the fairies assembled outside the barn. "I have dew, honey, and plenty of cream. At last I'm ready to—"

"Whip the cream!" said Rani. She quickly got to work whipping every drop of cream into fluffy mounds. When Rani was done, she looked around. "That's *more* than enough," she said.

Fairies always prefer whipped cream over plain.

With just a pinch of fairy dust, water-talent fairies like Rani can make magic with any liquid at all—not just water.

Fairies hate to see anything go to waste, so Lily suggested they take some of the extra whipped cream to Dulcie, a baking-talent fairy.

"As long as it's a quick trip," Tink added. She could hardly wait any longer for her tea.

"Lavender whipped cream! That goes *perfectly* with huckleberry shortcake," Dulcie announced when they arrived. "Tink, if you'll pick me some huckleberries, your cup of tea will have the perfect treat to go with it."

Tink pulled on her bangs in frustration. She just wanted to have a simple cup of tea. Then she thought about the sweet smell of huckleberry shortcake.

And so, Tink and Lily flew off to
pick a sack full of huckleberries.

Fairies take huckleberry shortcake very seriously.

The fairy who invented huckleberry shortcake has her own portrait in the Home Tree kitchen, and her Arrival Day (a fairy's birthday) is celebrated throughout Pixie Hollow.

At last, the berries were picked and the shortcake was made.

"*Now,*" Tink said, "I have dew and honey and cream . . . and even huckleberry shortcake! I'm finally ready to—"

"Have your cup of tea?" said Rani.

Tinker Bell stopped and looked around.

"No. Have a tea *party*!" Tink declared.

Tink's friends all agreed that a tea party was a wonderful idea.
"I know just where we should have it," said Lily. She flew off.
"And I know just what we should pack," said Dulcie. "Let's
take a trip to the pantry."

The basket-weaving-talent fairies pride themselves on their clever picnic baskets, with pockets and compartments for everything a picnic requires.

Dulcie puts a teapot in the center.

The walls and partitions of the basket are stuffed with dandelion fluff, to keep everything safe and sound.

The top opens wide for easy packing and unpacking.

Linens go on the bottom.

Dishware and cutlery go along the sides.

Note the pocket for star-shaped butter cookies.

The basket has multiple handles so fairies can share the load.

Linens fit for a tea party were the only things the fairies' pantry didn't have. So Beck flew off to the edge of the forest, where the Never spiders weave lace. She picked out the perfect lace for a tablecloth and five dainty napkins.

No fairy would ever dream of having
a tea party without lace for the table
(or toadstool)!

Lily, meanwhile, had flown off to get the fairy circle ready for the tea party. The fairy circle is among the fairies' favorite places to get together.

First, she coaxed a broad, red-spotted toadstool to serve as a tea table. Then, with a rustle and a wiggle, five smaller toadstools sprouted up to serve as fairy stools.

Then Lily made sure the fairy circle was bright with flowers. But one shy little flower bud didn't open.

"Time to bloom!" Lily said to the flower. She sprinkled a little extra fairy dust on it. At once, the bud sprang open so enthusiastically that a few petals flew off and drifted to the ground.

Lily's eyes lit up when she saw the fallen petals. She scooped them up and, in a wingbeat, fashioned a frock that would have made any fairy proud.

Garden-talent fairies have a special genius for creating clothes from nature.

Spiderweb-lace gloves are the perfect accessory for a tea dress!

Lily's sandals are dressier than her usual petal slippers, but they still allow her to feel the grass between her toes.

Just then, the rest of the party arrived at the fairy circle.

"Oh, Lily!" said Rani. "You look so beautiful!"

"Why, thank you," said Lily, with a blushing glow that shined nearly as orange as her new dress.

Dulcie opened up the picnic basket, and the fairies set the table.
"How should I fold the napkins?" asked Beck.
Lily said, "Don't forget the—"
"—spoons," Rani finished. "And the cockleshell cup is mine."

"At last," Tink said happily. Her cup twinkled at her brightly. She was finally going to have her cup of—

"Hmm," she said. "I feel like we're missing something,"

"Oh, my drips and drops!" Rani cried. "We're missing tea leaves!"

Milkweed-pod creamer

Almond-shell honeypot

Strawberry-seed scones

Huckleberry shortcake

"Shall I fly back for some?" asked Beck, ready to zip off to the Home Tree.

"No, wait!" said Lily. She reached into her pocket and pulled out a fragrant handful of bright green leaves. "I always like to keep a little mint from my mint patch close to me," she explained.

"Ah. Mint tea is my *favorite*!" Tink said.

Rani boiled the dew that she and Tink had collected. Then, Lily dropped her mint leaves into the waiting teapot.

When the tea was ready, Tink and her friends took turns pouring.

The time it takes a maple seed to spiral from the top of the Home Tree to the ground is exactly the time it takes a pot of fairy tea to brew.

Fairy tea-party etiquette has each fairy pour for the fairy on her left.

A simple moss tea cozy keeps the tea warm.

Tink reached for her cup. No sooner had she picked it up than Dulcie raised her hand to stop her.

"Wait!" said Dulcie. "Don't you think we should have a toast?"

"To who?" Tink asked.

"To you, Tinker Bell!" said Beck, lifting her cup and holding it high. "For bringing us together today—even if you didn't mean to!"

Tink gazed down at the beautiful little teacup she had made that morning. If she hadn't remembered her little piece of Never silver, she wouldn't even be here with all her friends.

She tapped the rim with her teaspoon and listened to the bright *ting!*

"To *you*," she murmured to the teacup. She took a sip of lovely mint tea, smiled, and sighed happily.